I AM READING

HOCUS POCUS HOUND

SAMANTHA HAY

Illustrated by

NATHAN REED

For Alice

KINGFISHER
An imprint of Kingfisher Publications Plc
New Penderel House, 283–288 High Holborn
London WC1V 7HZ
www.kingfisherpub.com

First published by Kingfisher 2006
2 4 6 8 10 9 7 5 3 1

Text copyright © Samantha Hay 2006
Illustrations copyright © Nathan Reed 2006

The moral right of the author and illustrator has been asserted.

A CIP catalogue record for this book
is available from the British Library.

ISBN-13: 9 780 7534 1307 4
ISBN-10: 0 7534 1307 8

Printed in China
1TR/0606/WKT/SCHOY/115MA/C

Contents

Chapter One

Marvo the magician was in a bad mood.

He was trying out his latest trick.

But it wasn't working very well.

"Stop fidgeting!" he shouted at his assistant Doris.

She was sitting inside a big box with just her head popping out the top, while Marvo tried to stick swords through the side.

"Sit still!" he thundered.

But Doris couldn't sit still. She'd swigged three extra-large milkshakes at lunchtime.

"Err . . . Marvo," she said. "I think
I need a wee!"

Marvo threw down the swords.

"Nincompoop! You're the worst
assistant in the world!"

Poor Doris.

She wasn't a very

good magician's

assistant.

She muddled up

the magic cards . . .

and mislaid the

magic wand.

And whenever she was sa<u>w</u>n in half
she'd fidget and squirm. (Secretly she
was a bit worried Marvo might decide
not to put her back together again!)

Marvo had had enough.

He yanked open the stage door.

"Follow me!" he shouted.

"The first person I see when I leave this theatre will be my new assistant!" But luckily for Doris, the street was empty . . . apart from a shaggy old dog eating scraps from a bin.

"He'll do!" bawled Marvo.

Doris was astonished.

"You can't have an old dog as your
assistant," she gasped.

But Marvo had decided.

The old dog was his new assistant.

And Doris was now dogsbody to

Marvo and his new assistant.

Chapter Two

The dog was quite ugly.
He was big and shaggy with grey
whiskers. And his coat was the colour
of mud.

Actually it wasn't just the colour of mud. It WAS mud! But Doris did her best with a large sponge and some of Marvo's shampoo.

The dog also had extremely bad breath, long toenails and a windy bottom. But Marvo didn't care. Because the old dog was sur<u>pri</u>singly clever!

So, while Doris sat and scrubbed rabbit poo out of Marvo's top hat, the dog learnt tricks.

He learnt card
tricks, hard tricks,
stand-on-a-box-
and-fly-tricks.

He learnt to
juggle with rings
and do tricks
with string.

16

He learnt to pull flowers out of his ears
and balance boiled eggs on his tail.
He never muddled up the magic cards
or mislaid the magic wand.
And he certainly never squirmed when
he was being sawn in half.

Marvo was delighted. "Who says you can't teach an old dog a new trick!" he boomed.

"I shall call him my Hocus Pocus Hound!"

The dog wagged his tail excitedly.

Then his windy bottom made a noise.

"People will come from near and far to see him!" said Marvo, holding his nose. And they did.

'Marvo the Magician and his Hocus Pocus Hound' was a sell-out!

"He's a million times better than you were!" bragged Marvo to Doris. "And I don't even have to pay him!"

Doris didn't mind. She'd never liked being Marvo's assistant anyway. And she'd always wanted a dog. Whenever Marvo wasn't looking, she'd swap the cheap tins of dog food that Marvo bought for extra expensive, super-size sausages.

Hocus Pocus Hound
was delighted.

Doris had a pet.

And Marvo had
loads of money.
And that's where
the tale might have
ended . . . fairly
happily ever after.
But then . . .
Marvo got greedy.

Chapter Three

One night, just before he and Hocus Pocus Hound went on stage, Marvo went to find Doris.

She was in the dressing room, shining Marvo's shoes.

"I've decided I don't need you any more!" he told her. "You're fired!"

Doris was stunned. "But who'll iron your cape and polish the wands?"

"Hocus Pocus Hound, of course!" said Marvo. "I can teach him to do anything."

But Hocus Pocus Hound, who was listening at the door, didn't like the sound of that!

He narrowed his eyes and growled.

But Marvo wasn't finished.

"And I know all about the sausages!" snapped Marvo. "I'll be taking the cost of them out of your last wages!"

And with that he swept out of the dressing room.

Doris was miserable.

With a heavy heart, she started to pack.

Meanwhile, Marvo and Hocus Pocus
Hound went on stage.

It was their best show ever.

Hocus Pocus Hound was on top form.

He balanced on a ball, while pulling
a cat out of a top hat.

Most daring of all, Hocus Pocus Hound allowed himself to be successfully sawn not in half, but in eighths.

The audience was delighted.

But Marvo wasn't finished yet.

Chapter Four

"Tonight," boomed Marvo to the audience, "my Hocus Pocus Hound will attempt a new trick – he will make ME disappear!"

The lights went down.

The audience was hushed.

Marvo stepped inside a big green box.

He waved to the audience, then pulled the door shut behind him.

Hocus Pocus Hound – beautifully turned out in top hat and tail – picked up Marvo's magic wand in his mouth, and trotted over to the box.

He bowed to the audience, then waved the wand three times in front of the box.

There was a puff of pink smoke, a
crash of thunder and a faint smell of
rotten eggs.

And suddenly the door of the box
creaked open. It was empty.

Marvo had gone. He'd completely
disappeared!
The audience was impressed!
There was thunderous applause.
People were on their feet.

Hocus Pocus Hound wagged his tail.

The audience cheered.

Hocus Pocus Hound wagged his

tail again.

The audience cheered some more.

But then slowly the cheering and the clapping stopped, as they waited for Hocus Pocus Hound to bring Marvo back.

But he didn't.

Instead, he lay down on the stage and went to sleep.

Chapter Five

The audience pointed and whispered and shuffled in their seats.

The theatre manager bit his nails and scratched his head.

But Marvo still didn't reappear.

Hocus Pocus Hound was now snoring.

There was only one person who could help. Doris!

The theatre manager rushed off to find her.

"Quick Doris! You've got to come!" he said, bursting into the dressing room.

But Doris had her coat on.

She'd packed her suitcase and was ready to leave.

"You can't go!" begged the theatre manager. "Hocus Pocus Hound has made Marvo disappear, and I don't think he wants to bring him back!" Doris tried not to laugh.

She rather liked the idea of a world without Marvo, but however much she disliked him, she didn't want the audience to go home disappointed.

Doris followed the manager back to
the stage. They found Hocus Pocus
Hound still fast asleep.
The audience was shuffling, and some
people were starting to leave.
"Wake up Hocus
Pocus Hound!"
said Doris,
tickling his ears.
Nothing
happened.

"Sausages!" whispered Doris.

But still Hocus Pocus Hound slept on.

The theatre manager was wringing his hands with worry.

Doris suddenly had an idea.

She took off Hocus Pocus Hound's top hat, and slipped it on her own head.

Then she whisked off her coat and turned to the audience.

"Ladies and gentleman!" she shouted.

"Please take your seats for the return

of the great Marvo the magician!"

Then she picked up Marvo's magic

wand.

She knew all Marvo's magic words!

She just hoped she'd remember them in

the right order.

After all, she didn't want to turn

Marvo into a mouse, or a frog . . .

(well, not really!)

She took a deep breath.

Then she waved the magic wand three

times in front of the empty green box.

Chapter Six

PHWOOOPH!

There was a puff of pink smoke, a crash of thunder and a faint smell of cheese.

Then suddenly the door of the box swung open . . .

. . . and there was Marvo!

A rather cross-looking Marvo!

"Wow!" thought Doris. "I've done it!"

"Hurrah!" shouted the audience.

They cheered and clapped so

loudly that they woke Hocus

Pocus Hound.

The audience was delighted.
People cheered and clapped, and
clapped and cheered, until finally the
curtain came down and everything
went quiet.

Marvo turned to Doris and Hocus Pocus
Hound with a face like thunder!

He opened his mouth to yell at them . . .

. . . when he noticed Hocus Pocus
Hound had picked up his magic wand,
and was waving it menacingly.

Doris had the same tough look on her
face as Hocus Pocus Hound.
Marvo suddenly felt a bit shaky.
His knees began to knock.
His throat felt dry.
He'd been lost in the green box for
rather a long time, and he didn't like
the idea of a repeat performance!

"Err . . . Doris," he said, "how would you like to be my assistant again?"

Doris blushed. "I'd love to!" she said.

"But what about Hocus Pocus Hound?"

"You can both be my assistant!" said Marvo, looking nervously at Hocus Pocus Hound. "I think perhaps two heads might be better than one!"

Everyone was happy.

Even with Hocus Pocus Hound's help,
Doris still sometimes muddled up the
magic cards and mislaid the magic
wand. But Marvo didn't shout at her
when she did.

Because Marvo knew, if he got even the slightest bit cross, Hocus Pocus Hound would give him a stern stare and a menacing wave of the wand. And Marvo knew what that meant . . .

About the Author and Illustrator

Samantha Hay trained as a
journalist and spent ten years
working in television. She now
looks after her wee girl and writes
children's stories. She lives in Wales.
'Hocus Pocus Hound' is her second
book for Kingfisher.

"I'd love to be a magician," says
Sam. "But unfortunately the only
trick I know is how to make
chocolate disappear!"

Nathan Reed has had a love for creating characters
ever since drawing in the sand with
his dad on holidays. He has been
illustrating children's books since
graduating from Falmouth
College of Arts in 2000. He now
lives in London.

"Although my own dog Sam is
very clever," says Nathan, "I don't
think he could ever perform tricks
quite like Hocus Pocus Hound!"

Tips for Beginner Readers

1. Think about the cover and the title of the book. What do you think it will be about? While you are reading, think about what might happen next and why.

2. As you read, ask yourself if what you're reading makes sense. If it doesn't, try rereading or look at the pictures for clues.

3. If there is a word that you do not know, look carefully at the letters, sounds, and word parts that you do know. Blend the sounds to read the word. Is this a word you know? Does it make sense in the sentence?

4. Think about the characters, where the story takes place, and the problems the characters in the story faced. What are the important ideas in the beginning, middle and end of the story?

5. Ask yourself questions like:
   Did you like the story?
   Why or why not?
   How did the author make it fun to read?
   How well did you understand it?

Maybe you can understand the story better if you read it again!